What if an Alligator Ate an Avalanche

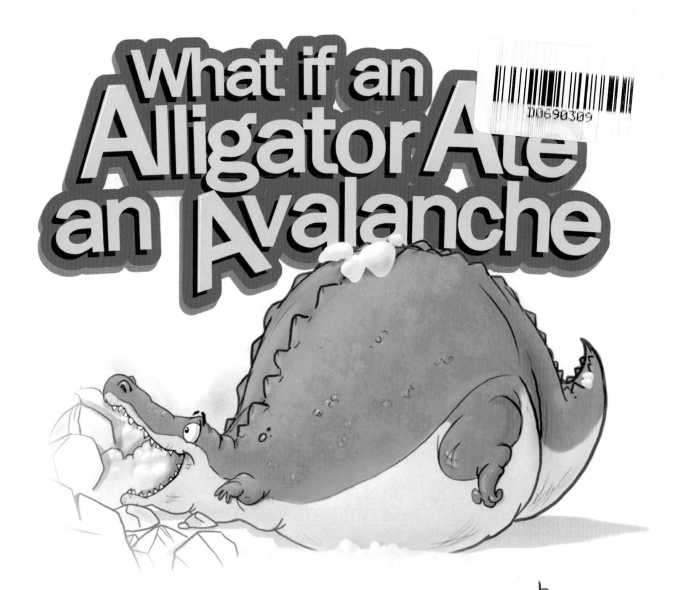

Author: Damien Macalino
Illustrator: Eduardo Paj

CRYSTAL MOSAIC BOOKS

Damien

Enjoy!

This is a work of fiction. All of the characters and events portrayed in this story are products of the author's imagination. Any resemblance to actual events or persons, living or dead, is entirely coincidental.

WHAT IF AN ALLIGATOR ATE AN AVALANCHE

Text and layout:
Copyright© 2013 Damien Macalino
Illustrated by Eduardo Paj

For information, address Crystal Mosaic Books,
PO Box 1276 Hillsboro, OR 97123
ISBN: 978-0-9836303-8-8

To my friend William.

Get Your Free Book!

Join the Super Secret Reader List and get a free copy of

The Wish Fish Activity Book

part of The Wish Fish Early Reader Series.

Super Secret Readers get free books, posters, videos, and all kinds of other great goodies, so hop on over to
www.macalino.com
and sign up today!

The adventure has just begun!

What if an Alligator ate an Avalanche

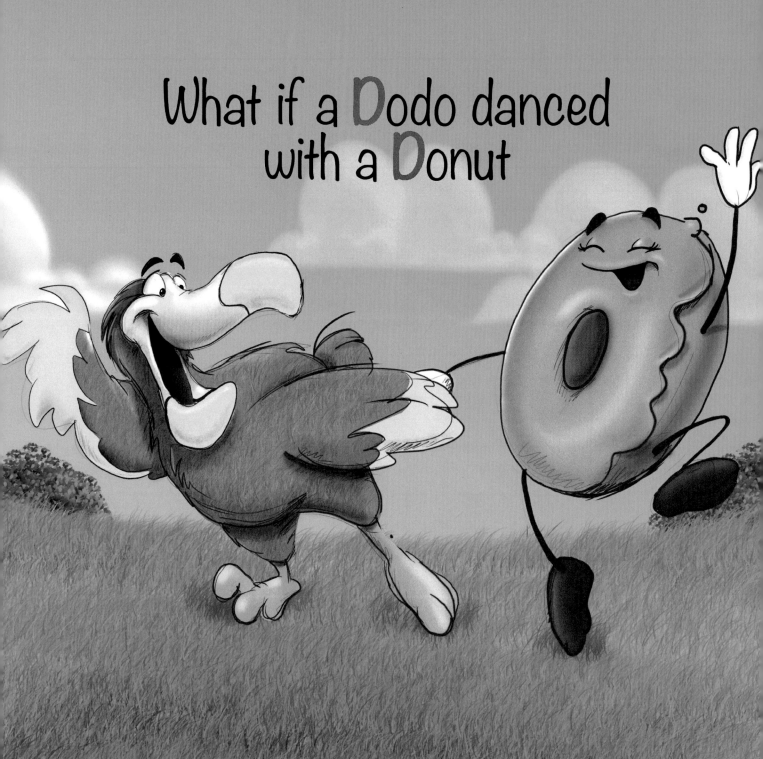

What if an Elephant sipped an Enormous Espresso

What if a Gorilla got Grumpy at a Gurgling Goose

What if an Iguana ice skated on an Ice rink

What if a marvelous
Mom marveled at a Mouse

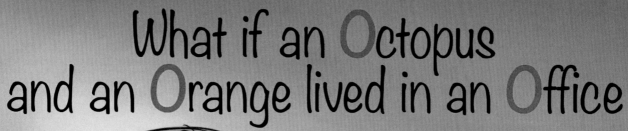

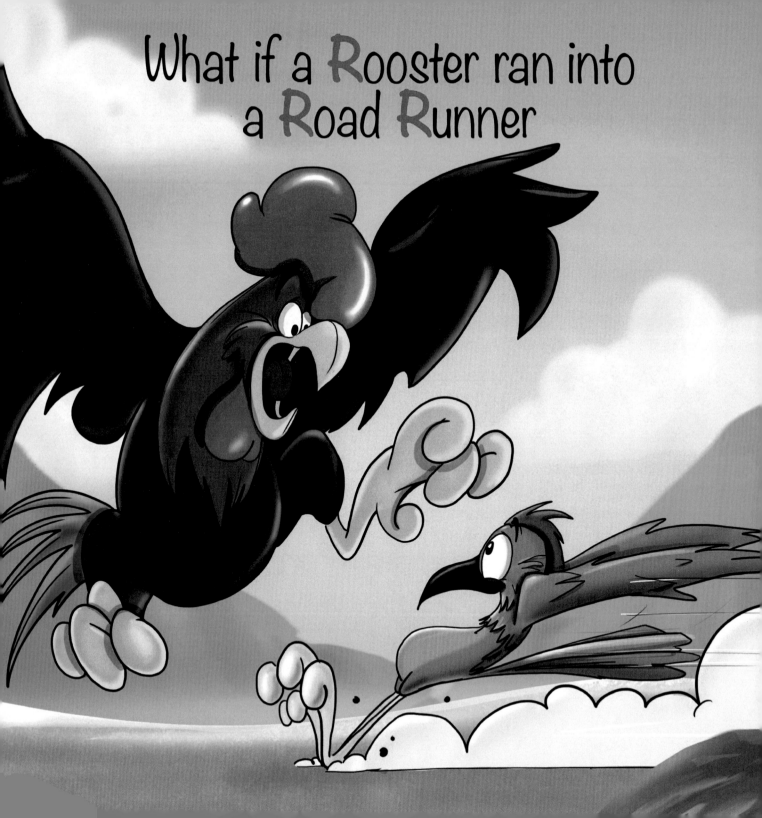

What if a **V**ulture vacuumed a **V**ampire bat

What if a **Walrus** waltzed
with a **Wicked Witch**

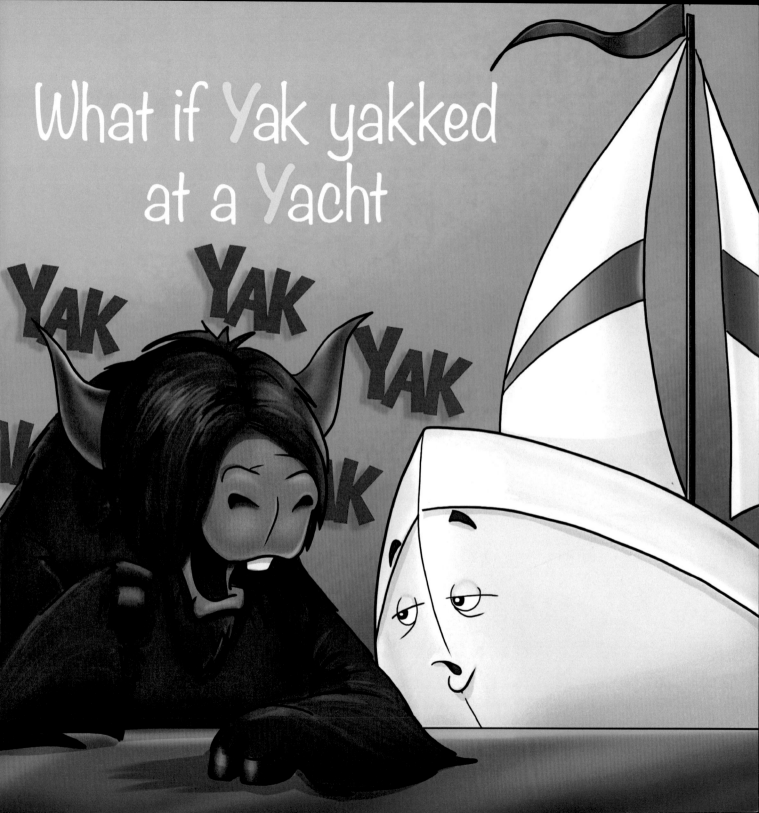

What if a Zebra zoomed on a Zip line

Get Your Free Book!

Don't let the adventure end!

Author: Damien Macalino

Damien is a 3rd grader living in Portland, Oregon with his family and his cat. When not working on his books, Damien can be found playing soccer or wall ball. He also enjoys reading and listening to other people's stories where he finds inspiration for his writing.

Illustrator: Eduardo Paj

Eduardo Paj is an independent graphic designer and illustrator specializing in 3D animation, character design, video post-production, and more. He is currently living in Querétaro, Mexico.

You can reach Eduardo at
http://www.behance.net/eduardopaj
http://eduardopaj.blogspot.mx/

40298875R00020

Made in the USA
San Bernardino, CA
17 October 2016